RUNNING BACK CONVERSION
I Was Barry Sanders

GORDON KORMAN

HYPERION PAPERBACKS FOR CHILDREN
NEW YORK

Printed in the United States of America.

First Edition
1 3 5 7 9 10 8 6 4 2

This book is set in 12-point Caslon.

ISBN: 0-7868-1237-0 (paperback)
Library of Congress Catalog Card Number: 97-71800

Contents

Laugh Attack

"The School Yard Elastic-Powered Net Bomb!"

A crowd gathered as quickly as ants on a dropped ice cream cone. The name of the new trick play was whispered excitedly around the circle of students. The Monday Night Football Club was already famous for their weekly sleep-overs to watch *Monday Night Football*. But they drew even more attention at Middletown Elementary School for their weird handoffs, wild passes, and breakneck tackles.

Nick Lighter was the quarterback. "Hut, hut, *hike!*" he barked.

Fellow club members Coleman Galloway and Elliot Rifkin were at wide receiver. As they ran out amid the jump ropes and hopscotch games, Nick dropped back to pass. But instead of throwing to his two running friends, he wheeled and hurled the ball with all his might into the school yard volleyball net. Like a slingshot, the mesh stretched back to its limit. Then it snapped forward, launching the ball high over Coleman's and Elliot's heads.

"Go deep!" cried Elliot.

The School Yard Elastic-Powered Net Bomb was catapulted past first Coleman and then Elliot. Both receivers ran harder.

"Look out for the bushes!" bellowed Nick.

Coleman, who was cautious, pulled up short. Elliot sprinted on snatching the ball out of the air. With no time left to stop, he barreled straight through the tall hedge that separated the school from nearby Wigwam Park. Some of the younger students clapped.

Nick sped up to a jog and raced around the bushes right behind Coleman. Elliot lay flat on his face on the grass. His clothes bore several rips from the sharp branches. He rolled over with a groan. His cheeks were scratched, and there were leaves in his hair.

He held up his arms, displaying the ball still clutched in both hands. "Touchdown!"

"You need the nurse, right?" Coleman asked nervously.

Elliot sat up and disentangled his legs from the greenery. "Only if she's going to conduct the postgame interview."

"I'll do it," said Nick. He held an imaginary microphone in front of Elliot. "Tell the viewers at home: what was going through your mind as you took on the unbeatable 'hedge defense'?"

Elliot played along. "Well, folks, I was thinking about the great Barry Sanders bulldozing through a line of three-hundred-pound defenders."

"And now, a word from our sponsor," Nick prompted. Monday Night Football Club interviews always included commercials.

"Right," said Elliot. "When I score my touchdowns, I'm always wearing my supercool Speed-of-Light sneakers. Each cleat is a tiny booster rocket, the same kind as they have on the space shuttle, so you're not just a football player—you're a piece of space-age technology!"

"Ha," snorted Coleman. "If you want to do a commercial for something, try Band-Aids."

Suddenly, Nick was wriggling like an earthworm and flailing his arms behind him. "Quick! Quick! Scratch my back!"

Coleman and Elliot both began scrubbing between Nick's shoulder blades.

"Harder!" commanded Nick. "Lower . . . to the left . . . aaaah!" He pulled up his jacket and shirt. "What's there?"

Coleman and Elliot looked. The source of the itch was a small pink bump right in the center of Nick's back.

"I think it's a mosquito bite," Coleman supplied.

"In November?" Elliot said in disbelief. "It snowed last night. There aren't any more mosquitoes around."

The bell rang to end recess.

"Hurry up," urged Nick, yanking his jacket back into place. "Mrs. Montrose promised to finish the last chapter of *Lucas and the Azure Forest*. I can't wait to hear how it all turns out."

" 'The evil armies of Gorok chased Lucas deep into the Azure Forest,' " read Mrs. Montrose. " 'For three days and nights he fled, hardly stopping to eat or sleep.' "

The students of 5A sat forward in their chairs. After two weeks, they had finally reached the exciting climax of this famous novel.

" 'But on the fourth morning,' " the teacher read on, " 'Lucas found himself encircled by Gorok's legions, pinned against the Endo-Barfian Ice Cliffs.' "

Elliot snapped to attention. Endo-Barfian Ice Cliffs? Endo-*Barf*ian? He fought off a snicker.

To his left, Nick began to make muffled vomiting sounds. Elliot clamped his hand over his mouth to keep from laughing out loud.

Mrs. Montrose was still engrossed in the story. "'And just when his doom seemed sealed, Lucas called upon his magic powers to turn himself into a ferocious lion—'"

"Psssst," whispered Coleman from the other side. "Endo-*Vomitonian!*"

A loud guffaw escaped Elliot. He covered it up with a severe coughing attack. "Cut it out!" he hissed.

Elliot was the smartest member of the Monday Night Club, but he had one weakness: he found anything gross to be amazingly funny. And once he started to laugh, it was like Niagara Falls. There was no stopping it.

"Endo-Blowing-Chow," Nick whispered to him.

"Endo-Technicolor-Yawn," put in Coleman.

A strangled sound came from Elliot. His face was bright pink.

"'. . . Lucas struck out from the cliffs and attacked the evil armies,'" read Mrs. Montrose in an emotional voice. "'He used the power of the lion to drive Gorok out of the forest forever. The end.'" She looked up from the book. "Well, what did you think? Let's have a class discussion. Just throw up the first idea that pops into your mind."

Throw up?! That did it for Elliot. He tossed back his head and howled with laughter, holding his sides as he rolled around in his chair. That sent Nick into a fit of giggles. Coleman closed his eyes and covered his ears. He knew that a single look or sound from either one of his two friends would be like a shot of laughing gas.

Mrs. Montrose's expression changed from surprise to anger. "Nick and Elliot," she said coldly. "You are both going to have to find a way to calm yourselves—out in the hall!"

No Such Thing as Magic

Outside the room it took a full five minutes for Elliot to get himself under control.

"That's right. Chuckle away," Nick said sarcastically.

"It's all your fault," gasped Elliot, wiping tears from his bright red cheeks. "Why did you and Coleman have to make those stupid jokes?"

Nick shrugged. "What's so hilarious about barf?"

"Don't make me laugh again," Elliot said sternly. "Mrs. Montrose already hates me for cracking up through the climax of that idiotic story."

"Idiotic?" Nick repeated. "I thought it was pretty cool."

"Get real," Elliot frowned. "How can that guy turn into a lion?"

Nick shrugged. "It makes it more exciting."

"That's not exciting; that's stupid," Elliot scoffed. "Let's say the Detroit Lions need a critical first down on

Monday Night Football. How much suspense would there be if Barry Sanders could just turn himself into a lion and eat the defense?"

"It's a totally different thing," Nick insisted. "Barry Sanders is a running back in real life. Lucas is a made-up guy with all these magic powers—"

"That's the biggest problem of all," Elliot interrupted. "Everybody knows there's no such thing as magic."

"What?!" Nick couldn't believe his ears. "How can you say that? Especially after what happened with my grandfather's football shirt?"

There was definitely something special about the ugly old jersey. It had been Nick's late grandfather's college football shirt during his years with the North Brainerd Eskimos. Last Monday night, Nick had been wearing it when he dozed off in front of the football game. While sleeping, *he'd actually switched places with John Elway*, the all-pro quarterback for the Denver Broncos! He'd played the entire game in the superstar's body while the real John Elway had spent those three hours as Nick, asleep in Coleman's attic.

"Look," Elliot began, "just because I can't explain how you ended up as John Elway last week doesn't mean it's the same thing as turning yourself into a lion."

Nick bristled. "Best friends don't call best friends liars. Are you saying you don't believe me?"

"I totally believe you," Elliot said quickly. "It's the magic I'm not so hot on."

"So how come you volunteered to try out the shirt next Monday night?" challenged Nick.

"Look," said Elliot. "Five thousand years ago, people thought the sun was driven across the sky by some guy in a chariot. Now we know better. Last week, you couldn't explain what made you John Elway, so you called it magic."

"Well, I wasn't exactly expecting it," Nick defended himself.

"But I will be!" Elliot exclaimed. "And if it happens to me too, I'll be all set up to figure out what makes the shirt work."

"If you wind up in the middle of a *Monday Night Football* game," Nick promised, "you won't have time to figure out two plus two. The ball zooms around like a bullet. Three-hundred-pound guys are flying in all directions. Thinkers get crunched into sawdust in the NFL."

The door to class 5A opened, and Coleman stepped into the hall. "What's going on? Are you guys talking about Monday night? You know I can't stand to miss stuff."

Nick pointed to Elliot. "The mad scientist thinks he *must* discover the secret of the Eskimos jersey."

Coleman shrugged. "Who cares why it works, so long as it does?"

Elliot snorted. "If Ben Franklin had said that about lightning, we'd be living with no electricity right now."

"Then where would we plug in the TV for *Monday Night Football*?" Nick smirked.

All three laughed.

"Where are we going to watch the games on Sunday?" asked Coleman.

"Count me out," sighed Elliot.

"Out?" gasped Nick. "How can you be out for football? It's impossible!"

"This is the weekend my Great-Aunt Leta comes up from Florida," grumbled Elliot. "Mom's inviting the whole tribe over—aunts, uncles, and millions of annoying little cousins. How about you let me keep the shirt at my place for a few days? I can study it. It'll keep my mind off my relatives."

"Okay," said Nick. "But remember, it's not your science project. Take good care of it."

"Trust me."

The Freak Show

Elliot's room looked like the statistics office at *Sports Illustrated*. Large poster boards covered every inch of wall space. On these, he recorded the team standings, the play-off races, and all sorts of player achievements.

Every morning, when he awoke, thousands of numbers smiled down on him—field goals, turnovers, first downs, interceptions, tackles, long bombs, penalties, and more.

Elliot loved numbers. They said it all. There was nothing mysterious about them. Not like the Eskimos jersey. He cast a sideways glance at the brown sweater hanging over the back of his desk chair.

How could a shirt make you switch bodies with a football player? It was as crazy as Lucas turning into a lion in that goofy book. Not that he doubted Nick. The guy would never lie about something this important. No one on earth took football as seriously as the founder of the

Monday Night Club. He even had the initials N. F. L. for Nicholas Farrel Lighter.

Elliot picked up the sweater and rolled the rough wool between his thumb and forefinger. He flipped open a steno pad and began making notes:

Color: brown, orange number (13)
Material: wool (world's itchiest)
Width: 29"—Height: 32"
Weight: .73 lbs.

There was a knock at the door. He stuffed the jersey into his desk drawer just as his mother stepped into the room. A giant lipstick smudge decorated her cheek. This was the badge of everyone who had been kissed hello by Great-Aunt Leta. Elliot had spent half the morning in the bathroom scrubbing the bright red gunk off his face.

"What are you doing up here?" she exclaimed. "Your cousins are arriving."

"Let me know when they leave, and I'll be right down," Elliot mumbled.

"Do you have to be such a sourpuss?" demanded Mrs. Rifkin. "I realize it's hard for you to care about people who aren't wearing football helmets, but these *are* your family."

Elliot folded his arms in front of him. "How many of them are crying?"

She frowned. "Why should any of them be crying?"

Downstairs, a frantic voice wailed. "Mommy! Brandon spit on the lasagna!"

"I was only *faking*, fathead!" shrieked another.

"And he called me fathead!"

"Welcome, Great-Aunt Leta," said Elliot with a lop-sided smile.

She hauled her son to his feet. "It's only once a year, Elliot. Let's go."

Downstairs was bedlam. Mr. and Mrs. Rifkin had five brothers and sisters between them, with a grand total of eleven children. Most of them were running away from Great-Aunt Leta, who was kissng and smearing at top speed. The rest were cowering under tables and chairs, and in corners. *It was like a cockroach infestation.*

All but one were a lot younger than Elliot. Twelve-year-old Leonard Rifkin was a seventh grader at Middletown Junior High. Leonard was the only person whose sense of humor was so idiotic that not even Elliot could find something funny in it.

"How's it going, ladies and germs? Put 'er there, Elliot, old pal!" Leonard held out his hand.

Reluctantly, Elliot shook it. There was a loud buzzing sound, and his palm was on fire with pain.

Leonard dissolved into hysterical laughter. "You fell for it!" he crowed. "You fell for my new joy buzzer! You should have seen your face!"

"I got the whole thing on tape," grinned Elliot's father from behind his video camera. "We can sue."

Elliot looked down at his palm, which was red and throbbing. "Big joke, Leonard."

"I know," gasped Leonard, out of breath from laughing. "I've got a million of them! Wait till you see!"

By the one o'clock NFL game, Leonard had mined all the couches with whoopie cushions, planted plastic spiders in the bathroom, set off a smoke bomb in the kitchen, and fed Great-Aunt Leta gag chewing gum that was laced with red-hot chili peppers.

"Turn up the volume, Leonard," called Elliot from the couch in front of the TV. "I can't hear anything over all that choking and spitting."

"I was only having a little fun," Leonard complained.

Elliot showed him the dark red mark on his hand. "You're such a barrel of laughs that I'm still in pain."

Sulking, Leonard slunk off, and Elliot turned his attention to the game between the Broncos and the Chicago Bears. Just the sight of John Elway made his spine tingle. Magic or not, the idea that last week that had been *Nick* was something amazing.

Tomorrow it could be Elliot.

A sudden fear froze him. What if the Eskimos shirt only worked with John Elway? The Broncos weren't playing tomorrow night. They were playing *right now!* Elliot could be missing his only chance.

He jumped up in a panic. He had to get into that sweater this instant! But—

The Eskimos shirt belonged to the whole Monday Night Football Club. Nick and Coleman would kill him if he attempted a switch without them!

What he needed was a preview. A test to see if he was missing out.

Elliot wracked his brain. How could he fall asleep just long enough to see if he was John Elway—but then wake up before the switch was complete?

Bzzzzzzz!!

He looked into the living room. Leonard was using his joy buzzer on their little cousin Katie. Enraged, the eight-year-old hauled off and punched Leonard in the stomach.

And suddenly, Elliot had the answer. "Hey, Leonard, let me borrow your joy buzzer."

"Don't try it on Katie," Leonard croaked in reply.

"She's got no sense of humor."

"But a great left hook," Elliot added with a grin. "Come on, fork it over."

With the buzzer in his pocket, he ran upstairs to his room and threw open his closet door. He gawked. Six-year-old Teresa Rifkin hung upside-down by her knees from the bar.

"Hi, Elliot," she greeted. "I'm practicing for my gymnastics meet."

"Well, do it someplace else," Elliot commanded. "Come on, beat it."

A small head poked out from under the bed. "Does that mean me too?" called Alex, another cousin.

"It means everybody," confirmed Elliot.

Alex wriggled himself free and followed Teresa out the door. "Don't forget Milo," he tossed over his shoulder. "He's hiding in your sock drawer."

"You promised you wouldn't tell!" came a muffled voice from the dresser.

"*Out!*" cried Elliot.

Finally, the coast was clear. Elliot dug the Eskimos jersey out of his desk and took it down the hall to his parents' room.

He paused inside the door. "All right, you've got five seconds to get out of here," he announced. "Then I'm bringing Great-Aunt Leta with a fresh tube of lipstick."

There were flurries of movement all over the room. Little cousins came from everywhere—behind the drapes, inside the wicker basket, even between the folds of Mrs. Rifkin's robe in the closet. Elliot herded them out and shut the door. Then he shrugged into the Eskimos shirt.

The Monday Night Football Club hadn't dubbed it the world's itchiest sweater for nothing. Wincing in discomfort, he turned on his parents' small TV. He took the joy buzzer and carefully taped it to the jersey, just above the number thirteen. If he could manage to fall asleep in the chair, his head would slump forward. His chin would hit the joy buzzer, and he would wake up.

His eyes fell on his father's video camera sitting on the dresser. At least Dad had given up on filming this freak show, he thought with a crooked grin. Which gave him an idea . . .

He reached over and pointed the camera at his chair. He hit Record. On TV, the Broncos were returning a kickoff. It was double-speed action. What a block! What a move!

Hey! he scolded himself. If he got hooked on this game, he'd never sleep. Mute the sound! Close your eyes! With effort, he sat back down and stretched out his legs.

He forced himself to concentrate on anything but football—Mrs. Montrose, *Lucas and the Azure Forest*, Nick's mosquito bite, the Eskimos sweater . . . hot, heavy, groggy, *drowsy*. . . .

As Elliot drifted off, a tiny glowing football appeared in the air just a few inches from his face. It looked almost like a firefly executing loop-the-loops. But there was something very special about the movement of the light as it danced above Elliot. It was tracing out a number: *20.*

The Trampoline-Block Pogo Punt Return

Food.

That was what Elliot saw. A giant dinner that would have fed a family of grizzly bears.

He found himself staring into a plate that was piled to the ceiling with turkey and mashed potatoes. A distant voice said, "Please pass the gravy."

Please pass the gravy?!

A loaded fork was coming toward him. He couldn't believe it didn't bend from the weight of all that turkey and cranberry sauce.

Cranberry sauce?! he thought in agony. *Oh, no! I hate cranberry sauce!*

As Elliot dozed off, his head slumped over onto his shoulder. Slowly, his chin began to slide forward, inching closer and closer to the buzzer.

Bzzzzzzzz!!

"Yeeow!" He leaped up out of the chair, grasping at his face.

Food?!

Well, he definitely hadn't been at the Bears-Broncos game—not unless they were snacking big-time on the bench.

He threw off the sweater in disgust. No magic there! Thanksgiving was coming up next week; he'd dreamed about turkey. Big deal! Except—

Why would his dream dinner include cranberry sauce, his least favorite food? The experience had been so real he could almost taste the fruity disgusting stuff at the back of his throat. Yuck!

He ran to the bathroom and began brushing his teeth at a frantic pace. In the mirror he noticed cousin Teresa chinning herself on the shower-curtain bar.

"What are you doing that for?" she asked him. "We haven't even eaten yet."

He spit into the sink. "Older people need to brush a lot more often," he told her. "Otherwise our teeth fall out and we have to wear dentures. When you get to be my age, you'll want to be careful about that."

She looked scared.

He caught sight of the red mark on his hand, and checked for a matching welt on his chin. He frowned. Nothing.

Just the faded pink impression of Great-Aunt Leta's kiss. What did that woman use for lipstick—permanent ink?

Come to think of it, his palm still stung from two hours ago, but his face felt fine now.

"Elliot! Teresa!" called Mrs. Rifkin from the kitchen. "We're ready to start serving!"

"Oh, wow!" cheered Teresa. "I'm starved!" She jumped down from the shower bar and ran for the stairs.

Elliot wasn't hungry in the slightest. If anything, he felt full. But he hadn't eaten since breakfast. Weird!

In his parents' empty bedroom, the video camera reached the end of the tape. It clicked off and began to rewind.

"That wasn't a dream," Nick insisted at recess on Monday morning. "You were a football player for a second."

The two friends were in the school yard waiting for Coleman. Nick was jumping up and down on his father's pogo stick, which was going to star in the Trampoline-Block Pogo Punt Return.

"All I saw in that dream was Thanksgiving dinner." Elliot told him. "It wasn't Thanksgiving. My mind must have been thinking ahead to next week."

"But you said it was a *huge* dinner," the bouncing Nick argued. "Pro players have big appetites. Man, you eat like a bird! Now, if we were talking about Coleman—"

Elliot grinned. "Coleman could eat a stegosaurus, not just a turkey."

"Hey, shut up," called Coleman. He steadied the school's small round trampoline over his head as he walked.

"Elliot tried out the shirt yesterday," Nick told Coleman.

Coleman's face fell. "Without *us*?"

"It was only a test." Elliot explained about his joy-buzzer wake-up call.

"Wow," said Coleman. "Who did you turn into?"

"I don't think I turned into anybody," Elliot sighed. "To be honest, it felt like an ordinary dream."

"What about the cranberry sauce?" Nick challenged. "Why would you dream about something you hate?"

"You don't have to like everything you dream," Elliot retorted.

"That's true," agreed Coleman. "I dream about math class all the time. Go figure." He turned to Nick. "Hey, how's the mosquito bite?"

"It had a baby," said Nick in disgust.

He pulled up his jacket and shirt. Now there were

two small red bumps in the center of his back.

"That's so weird," frowned Elliot. "*One* winter mosquito I can believe. But *two*?"

"Maybe both bites are from the same bug," suggested Coleman. "A real iron man hiding in Nick's room, waiting for spring."

"Go ahead, joke," snarled Nick. "I hope for Christmas you get stung by a winter hornet."

Elliot clapped his hands. "We're wasting time. Let's try the Trampoline-Block Pogo Punt Return."

The Monday Night Club got into position. Nick, the return man, went deep about twenty yards. He mounted the pogo stick and worked himself up to a slow bounce.

"Ready!" he called.

Coleman, the punter, started off the play. "Hut, hut, *hike*!"

As Coleman stepped forward to kick, Elliot, on defense, began his rush. He leaped onto the trampoline, launching himself high in the air. He threw up his arms to make the block.

Coleman punted. The football missed Elliot's fingertips by half an inch. It soared up at a steep angle above the tallest trees in nearby Wigwam Park.

"Short!" cried Coleman.

It was true. In order to get the ball past Elliot,

Coleman had punted high, but not far. The kick was not going to make it to the return man.

"I've got it!" shouted Nick, pogoing forward at top speed. He lurched and bounced to the spot where the ball was coming down.

It occurred to Nick at the last moment: there would be no way to make the catch without releasing the pogo stick. He was going to break his neck!

He let go of the handlebar and grabbed the ball just as the pogo stick struck a blue recycling barrel. The bin tipped over, spewing out cans, bottles, and newspapers. Nick did a swan dive into the pile of recyclables.

The other two members of the Monday Night Football Club came jogging up.

"No good," said Elliot sadly. "You made the catch, but not the runback."

"Awesome try, though," added Coleman.

"Hey, look!" Nick picked up a page from that day's sports section. The headline read: MYSTERY INJURY WON'T KEEP BARRY SANDERS FROM FACE-OFF WITH CHIEFS. Beside the story was a picture of the star running back with a round welt on the tip of his chin.

"How could he get that through his face guard?" mused Coleman.

Elliot took the article from Nick and scanned it.

"According to this, it's not a football injury. It happened sometime during Thanksgiving dinner."

"Thanksgiving dinner?" Coleman repeated. "That's not till next week."

Elliot snapped his fingers. "The Lions always have a game on Thanksgiving! So most of the players celebrate with their families the Sunday before."

"But that would be *next* Sunday," Coleman pointed out.

"Barry was serving dinner at a homeless shelter," Nick said. "And look!" Nick pointed from the newspaper picture to the hand holding it. Elliot's palm still bore a circular red mark from Leonard's joy buzzer. "These two scars are exactly alike!"

Elliot stared at him. "So?"

"Look," Nick began. "You should have a welt on your face exactly like the one on your hand. But you don't. Why not? Because you were Barry Sanders when you tried out the shirt! *He* got your welt; *you* got his turkey."

"That's crazy!" scoffed Elliot.

"Is it?" asked Nick. "You dreamed a Thanksgiving dinner." Who was having one at that very moment? Barry Sanders!"

"You mean," breathed Coleman, "*Elliot* ate Barry Sanders's dinner?"

"Just one bite," Elliot corrected weakly. This was

even harder to swallow than cranberry sauce!

"Don't you see what this means?" cried Nick. "Tonight, you're going to be Barry Sanders!"

Elliot took a step backwards. Barry Sanders! The greatest rusher in the NFL—his all-time favorite player! It would be a dream come true. But—

This was crazy! What about logic? What about reason?

"It—it just doesn't make sense," he managed in a small voice.

"It doesn't have to make sense," grinned Nick. "It's magic."

Magic. He was starting to hate that word. Still—Barry Sanders with a scar from Leonard Rifkin's joy buzzer? What other explanation could there possibly be?

As he got back to his feet, Nick lurched forward. "Whoa—"

Elliott grabbed hold of his shoulder and steadied him. "Are you okay? You took a pretty nasty spill before."

A funny look came over Nick's face. "I'm feeling kind of queasy."

"Maybe you should see the nurse," Coleman suggested.

Elliot laughed in his face. "You always think everybody should check into intensive care."

But Nick was very pale. "This time he could be right."

Flag on the Play

"I guess we should rethink the Trampoline-Block Pogo Punt Return," said Elliot as they headed for class after dropping off Nick at the nurse's office.

"It's too dangerous," agreed Coleman. "It's impossible for someone on a pogo stick to catch a football without falling off."

Elliot brushed his fingers along the row of lockers. "How about a swap? The return man uses the trampoline to jump up and make the catch; the punt blocker goes on the pogo stick."

Coleman shook his head. "Still too hard. What can he block with? His face? He needs his hands to hang on."

"True. Unless—," Elliot brightened. "The blocker wears a hat with a big piece of cardboard attached to it. We'll rename it the Pogo-Hat-Block Trampoline Punt Return."

"Pretty cool," Coleman approved. "Let's run it by Nick when he gets back."

Elliot led them into the classroom. "Nick's seeing the nurse," he told Mrs. Montrose. "He got kind of messed up at recess."

"What happened?" piped up Matthew Leopold, the class pest. "Did he jump off a cliff for one of your trick plays?"

"That will do," scolded the teacher. "We were talking about last week's fantasy stories based on *Lucas and the Azure Forest*." She handed Coleman his paper and then stopped in front of Elliot. Her smile was gone.

Elliot looked at his grade. "D-minus?"

"Ouch," whispered Coleman. "Even *I* got a C."

"We're studying *fantasy*," said the teacher. "Your paper was about Barry Sanders."

"That's *my* fantasy," Elliot replied stubbornly.

"I'll bet Barry Sanders can't turn himself into a lion," sneered Matthew.

"You're right," Elliot agreed. "Nobody can. There's no such thing as magic."

The teacher sighed. "I'll give you one more week to write a proper fantasy story. You don't want to be stuck with this D-minus dragging down your grade."

By noon, Nick still hadn't returned from the nurse's office. Coleman and Elliot rushed over at lunch.

"Oh, Nick's not here anymore," the nurse told them. "His father came by to take him to the doctor."

"The doctor?" Coleman was appalled. "Do you think he's really hurt?"

"No way," said Elliot. "You saw him. He just got his bell rung falling off that pogo stick."

After school they headed straight to the Lighter home.

Nick was in pajamas when he answered the door.

"Where were you today, man?" Elliot demanded. "What's with the pj's?"

"You've got another mosquito bite," added Coleman. "Right on the tip of your nose. And another one on your cheek."

"They're not mosquito bites," Nick said miserably. "I've got the chicken pox."

"On Monday night?" blurted Coleman.

Mr. Lighter appeared in the hall behind his son. "I don't think it matters to chicken pox what day it is," he said with a crooked grin.

"But Nick's okay for Monday Night Club, right?" Elliot persisted. "I mean, he can come to my house tonight?"

Mr. Lighter shook his head. "Chicken pox won't kill you, but it's nothing to fool around with. I'm afraid

Nicky's going to be stuck at home for the next few days."

"But what about *Monday Night Football*?" Coleman cried in agony. "We *can't* miss it! That would be like, you know, going for a week without breathing!"

"Couldn't we at least watch the game here?" Nick wheedled.

"That's a little selfish," Nick's father said disapprovingly. "You don't want to take a chance of making your friends sick."

"I won't get sick," Coleman put in. "I had chicken pox last year."

"And I had them when I was a baby," Elliot added quickly.

Mr. Lighter sighed. "Can't you boys play it safe just this week? After all, it's only one Monday night."

"*Only* one Monday night?" Nick repeated in disbelief. "Dad, there are just seventeen weeks in the whole NFL season!"

"And we won't live forever," added Elliot. "We'll be *lucky* if we get to see *Monday Night Football* a thousand more times before we die!"

"Plus we didn't start following football until third grade," Coleman picked up the argument. "Think about how many games we lost out on already. We can't miss tonight. It's not fair!"

"Why do you kids always say that?" demanded Nick's father. "Tell me you're disappointed, or upset, or even devastated. But please don't say it's not fair."

"Okay, so it's fair," shrugged Nick. "But it stinks! It's going to be torture! Total flaming-bamboo-under-the-fingernails *torture!*"

Mr. Lighter was close to surrender. "We'll see what Mom says," he decided, and escaped down the hall.

From her office, Mrs. Lighter set up a conference call with Mrs. Galloway and Mrs. Rifkin. The three reluctantly agreed that the Monday Night Football Club could be moved to Nick's house.

"But," Nick's mother informed him over the phone, "there's to be no leaping and wrestling and screaming tonight. You're sick, and you need your rest no matter how exciting the game is. Dad will be at work, and I'm meeting Aunt Sophie. Hilary will be in charge. So her word is law. Do you think you can listen to your sister just this once?"

"Absolutely, Mom," Nick agreed quickly. "Gotta go. Bye."

Coleman and Elliot exchanged high fives.

"That was some fourth-down audible you called," Elliot approved. "Talk about thinking on your feet!"

"Yeah, well, there was a flag on the play," Nick said

sourly. "Mom's leaving Hilary, Hilary, Heavy Artillery in charge."

"It won't be so bad," soothed Elliot.

"That's easy for you to say," Nick put in. "You're not even *really* going to be there. You'll be in Barry Sanders's body, stomping linebackers."

"We could use our secret weapon," Elliot suggested.

Coleman looked shocked. "I thought that was only in case of emergency."

"If Hilary gets on one of her bossy streaks, she'll ruin Monday Night Club," Nick promised. "What could be a bigger emergency than that?"

"I've got the secret weapon at my place," said Elliot. "I can smuggle it over when I go to get my sleeping bag."

The Secret Weapon

The secret weapon of the Monday Night Football Club was a foot-long piece cut from the narrow trunk of a small maple tree. Into the bark was carved H. L. & S. K. inside a heart. H. L. stood for Hilary Lighter. The S. K. was for Seth Kroppman.

Nick's eighth-grade sister had a huge crush on Seth. It had taken a lot of nagging to get him to carve their initials into the small maple. Unfortunately, Seth had worked his Swiss Army knife so deep that he'd killed the tree. Seth and Hilary had broken up on the spot. But before the city came to haul away the dead sapling, the Monday Night Football Club had sawed off the middle of the trunk. Someday, they knew, Hilary, Hilary, Heavy Artillery would push them too far. Then they could take out this secret weapon and threaten to flash it all around Middletown Junior High.

Elliot stood on tiptoe on his desk chair and felt around the top shelf of his closet for the rough bark of the maple. He brought down the secret weapon and hid it inside his sleeping bag. That someday, he thought, could be today.

Hilary Lighter's nickname, Heavy Artillery, came not from her size, but her personality. When Hilary wanted something, getting her to change her mind was like facing an armored division.

She was already rolling when Elliot got to the Lighter house.

"You're not getting pizza," she proclaimed. "You're sick. You need to eat healthy tonight."

"But we always send out for pizza," Nick complained. "It's a Monday Night Club tradition.

Elliot tossed his bedroll down in front of the TV. "He's got chicken pox, not pepperoni pox."

Coleman sidled up to him. "Did you bring the secret weapon?" he whispered urgently.

Elliot nodded. He shrugged out of his jacket, revealing the brown Eskimos jersey.

Hilary frowned. "I thought Grandpa's shirt was too scratchy for you guys."

"Oh—it's not so bad," Elliot said quickly.

"Well, it's a fashion nightmare," she decided. "You look like you've been chocolate-coated and rolled in owl feathers.

And anyway, how come you're wearing Nick's shirt?"

"How come you're not minding your own business?" Nick snapped at her.

"Hey, I know!" Hilary exclaimed. "There's this great new Vietnamese restaurant that just opened up. And guess what? They deliver!"

"Vietnamese—that isn't too spicy, is it?" asked Coleman. "I have a delicate stomach."

"Spicy is good for you," lectured Hilary. "It'll clear out your sinuses."

"His sinuses are fine, and so are mine." Nick folded his arms in front of him. "Why are we doing this? I mean, really? Does Seth Kroppman like Vietnamese food?"

Hilary picked up the phone. "Get real. I can't stand Seth Kroppman! He has no respect for the environment—hello, Saigon Kitchen?"

"Should I get the secret weapon?" hissed Elliot.

"Too early," Nick replied in a low voice. "We've got to save it for the game."

Actually, dinner turned out to be pretty good. The Monday Night Club had a lot of fun trying to pronounce the names of their food—like *muc chien* and *bo xao nam dong co.*

They stayed in the kitchen to do their homework. As usual, Elliot was finished first.

"What about your fantasy story for *Lucas and the Azure Forest*?" asked Coleman. "If you don't redo it, Mrs. Montrose is going to throw you off the Endo-Barfian Ice Cliffs."

Hilary looked up from her notebook. "That's in the book? Endo-*Barf*ian? Like throwing up?"

Elliot began to giggle. "Don't make me laugh," he managed. "Not on Monday night."

"It's not *that* funny," she commented.

"It is to him," said Nick, grinning. "Gross things blow his mind."

"Yeah?" Hilary was interested. "Like what?"

"Oh, the usual," Coleman began, "earwax, mucus, zits, athlete's foot, pus, drool—"

"Don't forget dandruff," Nick interjected.

Elliot was holding his sides, roaring with laughter. "No more!" he gasped. "I can't stand it! I'm out of here!"

He ran into the TV room. There, he unrolled his sleeping bag and lay back, using the bump made by the secret weapon as a pillow. He would *never* fall asleep if the guys kept on cracking him up all game long. They could be merciless. He remembered an entire Monday night where every five minutes Coleman had leaned over and whispered, "Jock itch." Elliot had woken up the next morning with his sides aching from laughing so hard.

This was it, then. He had to fall asleep *now, before* the game—while the others were finishing their homework. Otherwise he'd never see if this scratchy old shirt could do for him what it had for Nick.

He stared at the ceiling. It was impossible to relax.

Maybe he should count sheep. Nah. Too goofy.

So he started counting Barry Sanders's touchdowns. He remembered the first like it had happened yesterday—second down, goal to go, straight up the middle. And number two—a fifteen-yard scramble on a busted play. Number three was against Green Bay. . . .

The tiny glowing football appeared. It began to dance over Elliot's dozing form.

In the kitchen, Hilary, Hilary, Heavy Artillery jumped up and peered into the hall. "What the—"

"Something wrong?" asked Coleman from the depths of his science book.

"I thought I saw a light." She sat back down, frowning. "Like a match or something. But I must have imagined it. Hey, where's your Get-a-Life Club buddy?"

"Laughing himself out," shrugged Nick. "Come on, let's finish this stuff. It's almost time for *Monday Night Football.*"

Mr. Unstoppable

Dreaming, Elliot continued to count Barry Sanders's touchdowns.

. . . and the eighth was on that freezing cold day in Philly. And number nine was . . .

He frowned. *Two feet in front of me?!*

A large white *9* on a broad blue jersey bobbed up and down just ahead of him in a long cement tunnel. He froze, and someone bumped him from behind, knocking him over. He crashed to the hard floor.

Funny, he thought. *I can barely feel a thing.* He was padded from head to toe! He reached up to wipe his brow and nearly broke his hand on a football helmet.

Angrily, he craned his neck to see who had rammed him. "Why don't you watch where you're—"

His jaw dropped. He was chewing out none other than Herman Moore, the all-pro wide receiver for the Detroit Lions.

"Hey, man," Moore asked in concern. "Are you okay?"

"I—I—"

The big blue *9* squatted down in front of him. Elliot could see a matching *1* in front of it, making the number nineteen. It was attached to another famous face—Scott Mitchell, the Lions quarterback. Elliot gawked down the tunnel. There, at the end, roared Arrowhead Stadium, packed with cheering fans. It was *Monday Night Football*, and he was *here* — in Kansas City for the Lions' matchup with the Chiefs. Only he wasn't Elliot Rifkin anymore. He was . . . he was . . .

Mitchell hauled him to his feet and slapped him on the shoulder pads. "You're up, and you're feeling fine, right? Don't scare me, Barry."

Don't scare me, *Barry*.

It's true! Elliot marveled. *It's all true!*

He turned and ran back up the tunnel, slapping high fives with his bewildered teammates. He stopped in front of Bobby Ross, the Detroit head coach. "Coach, what's my name?"

Ross grimaced. "Not now, Barry. I'm busy."

Elliot darted into the locker room and stopped in front of the full-length mirror. His breath caught in his throat. Barry Sanders stared back at him—five foot nine, two hundred and three pounds of pure running dynamite.

The NFL's Mr. Unstoppable.

But Elliot's logical mind needed one final piece of proof that this miracle was really happening. He ran into the weight training room.

He slipped under a barbell that was loaded with three hundred pounds. Taking a deep breath, he grasped the handgrips and pushed. The huge bar lifted off its rack.

No way I'm this strong! Elliot celebrated. *I'm a monster! I'm Barry Sanders! It's amazing! It's incredible! It's . . .*

He wouldn't even allow himself to think the word, much less say it out loud. But for the first time, Elliot Rifkin couldn't deny it. He just might be faced with—*magic!*

"It's nine o'clock! I can't believe homework took so long!"

Barry Sanders woke up with a start. He looked around in alarm. What was he doing in this little room? What happened to Arrowhead Stadium? Why was he wearing this itchy shirt and not his uniform? Who were those two kids?

"Are you crazy, Elliot?" howled Coleman right in his face. "Why didn't you call us? We could have missed the opening music!"

Nick turned on the TV. Hank Williams Jr. was belting out the *Monday Night Football* theme song. Right!

That was the last thing Sanders remembered. He was in the tunnel heading out onto the field for the game against the Chiefs, and now he was here.

He frowned. Where was *here*?

Nick and Coleman were bouncing up and down on the couch, windmilling air guitars and singing along.

"Come on!" beckoned Nick.

Why would these crazy kids think he would want to jump on their sofa?

The music crashed to a finish. The TV screen went dark and, in the glass, Sanders caught a glimpse of his reflection. In horror, he sucked in air to the full capacity of both lungs.

He wasn't himself. He was some kid—just about the age of these other two! What was going on here?

Hilary ran into the TV room, waving her arms and yelling. The big eighth grader picked her brother bodily up off the couch and set him down on the floor. "Hey, none of that jumping around! You're sick! You've got to take it easy tonight!"

Nick glared at her. "Stay out of this, Artillery Hilary! It's a Monday Night Club thing!"

She folded her arms in front of her. "Who did Mom leave in charge—you or me?"

"That does it!" roared Nick. He turned blazing eyes

on the bewildered Barry Sanders. "All right, Elliot. Show it to her!"

The star runner looked back blankly. Elliot? Who was Elliot? "Show what to who?" he asked weakly.

Nick stared at him in disbelief. "You know, the *thing*! The *you know what*!" He dropped his voice to a whisper. "The secret weapon."

But Sanders was no longer paying attention. He was staring in horror at the TV screen, where something very strange was happening.

Barry Sanders was watching *himself* take a handoff on *Monday Night Football*!

The Blabaholic

It was like the whole universe was a hundred yards long, held together by a shell of seventy-nine thousand screaming people. Only giants lived on this turf, and life took place in crazy flying spurts whenever somebody yelled . . .

"Hut!"

Elliot snatched the football and tucked it under his arm. With Barry Sanders's legs, every single step felt like a cannon shot. He wheeled and dashed up behind the Detroit offensive linemen.

Oh, no! he panicked. *I'm running right into the heart of the defense!*

He tried to put on the brakes, but could not slow down. He felt like he was being operated by remote control. His feet had a mind of their own.

I'm going to get creamed—

At the last second, a gap opened up beside the left tackle. He exploded through the hole like a leaping panther.

Man, how did I do that?

A red shirt lunged to tackle him. Elliot cut to the right, but the linebacker grabbed a fistful of jersey and hung on, pulling Elliot downward.

Now what? he asked himself. But Barry Sanders's body knew exactly what to do.

He spun around, twisting free. Another linebacker hit him. He staggered sideways but would not fall. As he struggled to stay upright, he felt arms of iron clamp around his waist.

That's it! I'm toast!

Desperately, Elliot began pumping his powerful legs like pistons. Slowly, he began to move forward, dragging the tackler right along with him.

Elliot felt an excitement that shook him down to his cleats. This was what made Barry Sanders the most feared runner in the NFL. This was what made him Elliot's all-time number one hero. *You can't knock me down!* he wanted to howl. *I'm Barry Sanders!*

There was a gasp in Arrowhead Stadium as he passed the first-down marker.

POW! The free safety hit him like a guided missile. The defender's helmet struck the ball, popping it out from the crook of Elliot's arm.

Fumble!

Elliot dove but he was too late. Another Chiefs player hurled himself onto the bouncing football. First down, Kansas City.

Elliot was devastated. He had blown the drive for Detroit.

He expected his teammates to be furious. Instead, they were patting him on the helmet and shoulder pads as the defense took the field.

"Nice moves," Mitchell told him.

"But I fumbled!" he cried in agony.

The quarterback looked at him in surprise. "Take it easy. Most of the time you don't."

Elliot took no comfort. He knew the NFL was exciting, but he never expected it to be so *hard*, even for a guy like Barry Sanders.

Learn the play, remember the snap count, follow your blocker, stay upright, fight for the first down, *hang on to the ball*! Elliot wondered if he would ever get it right.

The Chiefs kicked a field goal to take a 3–0 lead.

"Keep your voice down!" snapped Nick. "We're trying to watch a football game!"

Hilary was flaked out on the couch of the TV room. The portable phone seemed like it was attached to her head. She was talking her way through *Monday Night Football*.

"She sure has a lot of friends," commented Coleman.

Nick was totally disgusted. "Listen to her blab. It's a blabathon! She's a blabaholic!" He turned to the guy he took to be his friend Elliot. "If you'd remembered to bring the secret weapon, we'd have Hilary, Hilary, Heavy Artillery off our backs."

"Sorry," Barry Sanders could only shrug. Compared with the shock of being turned into an eleven-year-old stranger, this secret weapon was the least of his worries.

"Hey, I heard that!" called Hilary. "What secret weapon?"

"Watch what you say," Nick whispered. "She has ears like radar."

"I heard that, too!"

"It's hot in here," complained Sanders. He began to pull off the Eskimos jersey.

Horrified, Nick and Coleman pounced on him and yanked the sweater back over his head.

The star runner gawked at them. "What are you—nuts?"

"*We're* nuts?" Nick repeated. "You need that sweater to—" He peeked over his shoulder. His sister was looking straight at them. "I mean, you can't—*you know*—unless you're wearing the sweater."

"Shouldn't you be falling asleep by now?" added Coleman. "It's almost the end of the first quarter."

Sanders was completely cowed. These kids belonged in the insane asylum! He wanted to do something—to take some kind of action. But what?

He didn't dare call the police. Who would believe his story? That he, a boy, was really the top rusher in the NFL. *He'd* be the one to end up in the nuthouse! Besides, that Heavy Artillery person was hogging the phone. Her brother was right. She really *was* a blabaholic!

All he could do was watch himself on TV—and hope and pray that all this turned out to be nothing more than a bad dream.

Touchdown, Barry Sanders

GOODYEAR.

Elliot gazed up at the blimp over Arrowhead Stadium.

I'm not watching TV, he reminded himself. *I'm seeing it in real life.* Awesome.

The huge crowd erupted with boos every time he touched the football. At first, Elliot was insulted. But then he found it kind of flattering. After all, these were Kansas City fans. And who was more dangerous to the Chiefs than a fifteen-hundred-yard rusher? Elliot ignored the catcalls and concentrated on the Detroit cheerleaders, who were spelling out his name.

Well, Barry Sanders's name.

The Chiefs led 10–0 and Detroit was playing catch-up. Elliot was trying out Sanders's famous stutter-step for big gains. One day he'd be able to look at the charts on his bedroom wall and know that some of those yards were his. But today the scoring plays just weren't coming.

"Fourth down!" called the referee.

Elliot was dying to go for it. He could make it! He knew he could!

I'm a player now, not a fan, he reminded himself. *I have to have faith in the coach.*

Bobby Ross decided to kick a field goal, making the score 10–3 Chiefs.

"Sometimes patience is more important than guts," the coach explained. "Maybe our defense can come up big for us."

The strategy paid off. On the first play of the Kansas City drive, quarterback Elvis Grbac dropped back into his own end zone to pass. Suddenly, the Lions' Reggie Brown broke free of his blocker. The star linebacker charged Grbac and sacked him for a safety. Elliot leaped up and down on the sidelines, waving a towel above him like a helicopter blade. That meant two points for Detroit. *And* the Lions would get the ball back.

Elliot was vibrating with excitement as he took his place in the backfield. This was Lions football—making opponents pay for their mistakes.

"Hut!"

Elliot took the pitch on the run. Up ahead, the Kansas City defense looked as solid as armor plating. He put down his helmet, determined to bull ahead for a yard or two. He closed his eyes and prepared for a collision that would jar his back teeth loose . . .

. . . but it never came. Surprised, he opened his eyes. He was past the line, charging through the open field.

Wow! he celebrated. *This is going to be a big gain!*

Herman Moore knocked the cornerback flat on the turf. Johnnie Morton also threw a beautiful block.

It hit Elliot like a bolt of lightning. All the speedy defenders were out of the play! He had a clear path to the end zone!

The angry cries of the home crowd were like a jet engine strapped to his back. He flew down the field, crossed the goal line, and spiked the ball.

The referee raised his arms. "Touchdown!"

Elliot was mobbed by his teammates. His head was knocked every which way by helmet-bonks of congratulations.

"Lions rule!" he howled, delirious with happiness.

"Hey, Barry," came the calm, amused voice of Scott Mitchell. "The game's not over yet."

"Sorry," said Elliot in embarrassment.

It's hard to act like a pro when you're really the biggest fan in the world caught in a dream come true—a chance to star in a Monday Night Football *game!*

On the Detroit bench, Coach Ross was holding up two fingers.

Elliot's breath caught in his throat. The crowd grew quiet with anticipation. The Lions were going to go for a two-point conversion, one of the toughest plays in football!

The Perfect Souvenir

The Detroit offense lined up on the Kansas City three yard line. In his stance in the backfield, Elliot wished he could hear what the *Monday Night Football* commentators were saying on TV. He pictured Frank Gifford explaining that the Lions had a single chance to get the ball into the end zone for the two-point play. He thought of Nick and Coleman in their sleeping bags, watching and knowing that their best friend was right in the middle of it all.

"Hut!"

Elliot burst forward and reached for the football . . .

. . . and grabbed thin air! It was a fake handoff! Mitchell faded back to pass.

Suddenly, red shirts were everywhere. The Chiefs were blitzing! It was a gutsy call! Elliot spotted a charging linebacker with a clean shot at Scott Mitchell.

It was up to Elliot to protect his quarterback. He hurled himself at the defender.

Crash! The collision knocked Elliot flying, but the linebacker was still on his feet. Out of breath, Elliot scrambled to his knees and put his shoulder into the pass rusher's stomach.

"Oof!" The big man was stopped in his tracks.

Mitchell reared back and fired a perfect strike to Herman Moore. The two-point conversion was good!

And my block made it possible! Elliot celebrated. *There's a lot more to football than what you see on highlight films.* It took a team effort.

The gun went off to end the first half. The Lions had come from behind to take the lead, 13–10.

The locker room at halftime was a blur of clipboards and tape. Coaches mapped out plays while trainers taped up equipment, ankles, knees, shoulders, wrists—*there isn't a single body part that these guys won't tape,* Elliot noted.

Some of the Lions were studying Polaroid photographs of plays from the first half. The pictures were taken both from the sidelines and from a special booth high up in Arrowhead Stadium. Elliot examined his surroundings. There was definitely a lot of camera equipment around—everything from high-powered zoom lenses and state-of-the-art video recorders to simple Polaroids.

He smiled. To Elliot, photography was for vacation

pictures, not serious football strategy. On the other hand . . .

What real-life trip could be as exciting as the adventure I'm in the middle of right now? he asked himself. *If there ever was the perfect moment for a souvenir snapshot, this is it!*

He took one of the Polaroid cameras, carefully aimed it at his locker, and set it for time delay. Then he scribbled a quick message on a clipboard and held it up.

Click!

"Is this going on the cover of *Sports Illustrated*?" came the amused voice of one of the trainers.

"Sorry." The last thing Elliot wanted to do was get Barry Sanders in trouble. "We're not supposed to take pictures, right?"

"Gain fifteen hundred yards again this season," the man laughed, "and we'll let you carve your face onto Mount Rushmore."

Grinning sheepishly, Elliot waved the instant photograph in the air. When it was fully developed he handed it to the trainer. "Do me a favor. Mail the picture *here*." Quickly, he wrote his home address on the clipboard. When Nick and Coleman saw this photograph they'd totally freak! "The sooner the better!"

"Sure thing, Barry," agreed the man. "But who's Elliot Rifkin?"

"Just a kid," Elliot replied. "But he's such a big fan that sometimes I think he's almost a part of me!"

The trainer got an Express Mail envelope out of the small office area. Watching him, Elliot's eyes fell on the telephone. Why didn't he call Nick's house right now? It would blow Nick's mind to hear Barry Sanders's voice on the other end of the line.

He dialed zero, then the Lighters' number. "Collect call," he told the operator. "My name? Barry. Barry Sanders."

"Yeah, right," the operator snorted. "Who are you calling, Michael Jordan?"

Elliot's brow furrowed. "Could you just connect me, please? Coach Ross will kill me if I miss all of half-time."

The call went through. He frowned at the busy signal. Had Nick and Coleman gone crazy? What kind of an idiot would be on the phone on Monday night? And what conversation could be so important that it was worth missing the highlights of the week on *Monday Night Football*?

"Exactly!" Hilary exclaimed into the receiver. "So I said to that creep, 'Yo, Seth, anybody who could kill an innocent tree is no boyfriend of mine.' And then *he* said—"

"Will you please shut up?" Nick pleaded. "The second half is starting!"

"Go scratch your chicken pox," Hilary retorted.

"Come on!" Nick reasoned. "What if someone's been trying to call us for the last hour and a half?"

"Yeah, right," laughed Hilary. "I'll bet Barry Sanders has been trying to phone us just to say hi."

"What could you know about Barry Sanders?" snarled Nick. "You couldn't follow a football game. It takes *intelligence*!"

"Marilyn, I'll call you back," said Hilary, and hung up the phone. "I know more than you think, doofus." She pointed at the screen. "See, that's him right now. Number twenty. He lines up behind everyone else. And he has a really cute smile on TV commercials. So there!"

The ball was snapped. Number twenty burst through the line, hurdled a tackler, and rambled for a fifteen-yard gain.

"Wow," breathed Hilary. "He's pretty good, too. He smashed through all the crouching guys."

"They're called *linemen*!" Nick muttered. "And they're not crouching. The rules say they have to start from a down stance!"

"I think they're just too big to stand up straight,"

Hilary suggested. "It can't be easy when you weigh three hundred pounds. Look at the dinosaurs."

"They're the best blockers in football," Sanders came to the rescue of his teammates. "Watch the replay. The guards push their men in opposite directions. That's what makes the hole for me—I mean him—I mean Barry Sanders."

Hilary got up off the couch and joined the Monday Night Football Club on the floor in front of the TV. "Maybe there's more to this football junk than I thought. It's really sweet that they have a group hug before each play."

"It's called a *huddle!*" seethed Nick. "And it's serious business. There's nothing sweet about it."

Coleman sidled up to Barry Sanders. "Hey, Elliot," he whispered. "Why are you wasting your time talking about the game when you could be in it?"

The superstar stared at him. "You know about that?"

"You have to go to sleep," Coleman insisted. "Don't be crazy and miss your chance."

Sanders sighed. *Something* was definitely crazy here. But sleep had nothing to do with it.

"It's starting to rain in Kansas City," Nick observed. "I wonder how that'll affect the game."

"The ground gets muddy," said Sanders. "Your cleats kind of rip up the turf—"

Suddenly, he realized that Nick, Coleman, and Hilary were regarding him oddly.

"Or so I've heard," added Sanders.

Ninety-Seven Long Yards

The same things that made NFL football exciting could make it agonizing in the wink of an eye. Just when it seemed as if the Lions were taking over, Elvis Grbac showed why he had earned the quarterback's job in Kansas City. He hit a streaking receiver with a seventy-yard touchdown pass. In the gloomy winter drizzle, Detroit trailed once again, 17–13.

We can get it back, Elliot told himself. *We're the Lions.*

At that moment, there was a flash of lightning and a crack of thunder. The skies opened up, dumping a heavy drenching downpour onto Arrowhead Stadium. Fans scrambled to put up hoods and protect themselves with programs and newspapers. Coaches and players shrugged into capes and parkas. The officials pulled a tarpaulin over the rack of extra footballs. On the field, Elliot was pummeled by sheets of blowing water. The sound of heavy raindrops echoed inside his helmet like machine-gun fire.

The game took on a wild tone. Players slipped and slid. Passes were dropped. Every tackle churned up a muddy tidal wave. The ball became wet and heavy. It was difficult to throw, even harder to catch, and almost impossible to run with. In spite of Barry Sanders's great strength, Elliot felt like he was carrying an anvil.

If this was baseball, we'd be in a rain delay. Not even a typhoon could stop an NFL game. But how were the Lions ever going to score in this mess?

Both teams sputtered and sloshed through the fourth quarter. Then, with only 2:37 to play, disaster struck. Slipping and tripping on the muddy turf, the Lions blockers were turned around and confused. This gave Dan Saleaumua, the all-pro defensive end, a clear shot at Scott Mitchell.

Wildly, Elliot hurled himself into Saleaumua's path. He felt a shoulder like a battering ram explode into his chest. Gasping, he fought to keep Saleaumua away from the quarterback. But the future Hall of Famer reached out a sledgehammer fist and pounded down on the ball in Mitchell's hands. The fumble hit the wet ground and took a funny bounce, dancing across the field. Seventy-nine thousand gasps sounded like they had come from a single megapowered throat. Elliot could feel the ground shake as twenty-two huge NFL players stampeded after the loose ball. He hurled himself into the pileup, fighting the snarl of grasping hands.

"We've got it!" yelled a Chief.

"No, *we've* got it!" Elliot cried automatically. In truth, he didn't have the slightest idea where the ball was.

The officials began separating bodies. And when they got to the bottom of the pile . . .

"Kansas City football!" barked the referee.

Three plays later, the Chiefs kicked a field goal. The score was now 20–13. The two-minute warning sounded.

"Nobody panic!" roared Ross on the sidelines. "We can tie it up and win in overtime!"

But when the Detroit kick returner slipped in the mud and fell on the three yard line, Elliot thought panic sounded like a pretty good idea. In the huddle, he peered bleakly over Mitchell's head at the end zone, ninety-seven long yards away.

It might as well be fifty miles, he thought. *It's impossible to move the ball in this lousy rain!*

"Okay," said Mitchell in a low voice. "We're backed up too far to pass in this weather. Barry, it's up to you."

To me? I'm eleven years old! I'm a fifth grader at

Middletown Elementary School! How can the fate of the great Detroit Lions possibly be up to me?

Elliot was too terrified to speak. So it must have been a little piece of Barry Sanders that replied, "No problem, Scott. Just give me the ball."

It was a classic confrontation—a star running back against a great defense. The whole game boiled down to this: four bone-crushing runs, two measuring sticks. There was dead silence in the stadium as the officials stretched out the chain.

"I never knew you bit your nails, Barry," Mitchell commented mildly.

Elliot held his breath. *It's not enough. I've let my teammates down. I'm not worthy to be a great star like Barry Sanders—*

He stared. *Wait a minute!* The nose of the ball was *just* touching the back of the pole. It was only by a hair, but—

"First down!" called the ref, pointing forward.

The drive was alive.

"And if you're just tuning in," announced Al Michaels on *Monday Night Football*, "you've been missing something amazing! Barry Sanders has lifted the Detroit offense onto his shoulders!"

"He's fantastic!" Hilary declared. "He started way, way back by his own big antenna-thingie!"

"They're called goalposts, Miss Football Expert," snarled Nick.

"It's a good thing you didn't fall asleep," Coleman whispered to the real Barry Sanders, who sat, stunned, in Elliot's pajamas. "No way you could pull off what Barry Sanders is doing right now."

"Oh, yeah," agreed Sanders weakly. "No way."

On TV, number twenty spun away from a tackle. The move added ten yards to a big gain. All four cheered themselves hoarse.

"Way to go, Sandy!" applauded Hilary, her eyes riveted to the screen.

"*Sandy?!*" Nick repeated. "What are you, his mother? 'Barry' isn't familiar enough for you?"

"As a fellow athlete, I feel a special connection between us," Hilary retorted. "I can relate to Sandy as well as if he was right here in this room."

Sanders stared at her. Did the girl have ESP or something?

"Sure, why not?" Nick said sarcastically. "He's an NFL superstar, and you play junior high volleyball. You're practically teammates!"

"But Sandy's a *girl's* name!" Coleman protested.

"Don't be sexist," Hilary scolded. "Sandy isn't insecure about his manliness like you wimps. What I can't figure out is why he always runs *through* the defense, not around it."

"No one has enough speed to get outside on every carry," protested Sanders himself.

She scowled at him. "You don't know diddly-squat about Barry Sanders! He's slippery. He can always cut back if he sees a good spot to run through. The players move, and different openings come and go."

Sanders looked surprised. "I never thought about it that way."

Nick glared at his sister. "You've watched a grand total of half a game, and now you're the great coach Vince Lombardi? Football isn't that simple. The Lions can't let Sanders do it alone. There's less than a minute left on the clock. They need a big pass play!"

"I can do it," said Sanders, his eyes riveted to the game.

"*You?!*" chorused Nick, Coleman, and Hilary.

"I mean *he* can do it!" Sanders insisted, pointing at the TV. "I mean Barry Sanders! I mean—look!"

On the screen, number twenty took the handoff from Mitchell. But instead of wheeling downfield, he stopped and spun around. He cocked back his arm and unleashed a long bomb.

"Halfback option pass!" cried Nick and Coleman.

"Halfback *what*?" Hilary stammered.

The ball sailed high and wobbly through the rain at Arrowhead Stadium. All at once, the throw seemed to lose power in the strong wind. It dropped steeply back to earth.

"I can't look!" shrieked Hilary.

From a crowd of Chiefs leaped Herman Moore. He rose above the cornerbacks and safeties, and snatched the ball out of the air with hands of iron. He hit the turf running, pushing away tacklers with a stiff arm. When they finally wrestled him down, he was on the one yard line.

"There's only thirty seconds to play!" cried Hilary in anguish. "Why don't they call time-off?"

"Time-*out*!" corrected Nick.

"Coach is saving it," Sanders said excitedly. "He wants to stop the clock if we don't score here!"

He crawled right up to the TV set with the three kids. In spite of everything, he was sucked into the drama of the game. Suddenly, his worries over getting his old self back were moved to second place behind a more pressing question: could the Lions—and the mysterious impostor who seemed to be *him*—send this game into overtime?

* * *

The crowd noise in Arrowhead Stadium drowned out the thunderstorm. The fans howled their support of the defense. A goal-line stand here would guarantee the Chiefs a 20–13 victory.

But the Lions were so focused on the end zone that they barely noticed the screaming people or the pouring rain. Unblinking eyes bulged with pure concentration.

The Chiefs nose tackle had been injured on the last play. The clock stopped, and then started again when his replacement jogged out onto the field. His clean white pants stood out like a sore thumb. The other twenty-one players were mud from head to toe.

"Watch out for this new guy," Scott Mitchell whispered in the huddle. "He's only a rookie, but he was an all-American in college."

Elliot regarded the big newcomer. He was huge, even for a lineman. He turned around, and his massive back seemed to block out half the end zone. Elliot read the name above the number on the rear of his jersey: O'BARFSKY.

Heartbreaker

Elliot stared at the rookie. He gawked. He goggled. *O'Barfsky?!*

And then Elliot Rifkin laughed. Standing on the one yard line in the rain, he threw back his head and howled. He forgot the score, and the fact that the clock was running. All he could think of was O'Barfsky. *O'Barfsky!*

"Barry! Line up!" barked Mitchell.

But Elliot was out of control. His shoulder pads shook with the trembling of his hysterics. O'Barfsky! He could almost hear the voices of Nick and Coleman, egging him on. O'*Barf*sky! O'*Vomit*sky! O'*Throw-Up*sky!

An unpleasant growl came from the throat of O'Barfsky.

"There seems to be something wrong with Barry Sanders," announced Al Michaels in the broadcast booth. "But I can't make out his injury—"

"Injury, my foot!" said Dan Dierdorf in amazement. "It looks like he's *laughing*!"

The clocked ticked down. Ten seconds . . . nine . . . eight . . .

"What's going on out there?" bellowed Ross from the bench.

"Are you crazy, Barry?" shouted Mitchell. "Get in the backfield!"

Elliot barely heard him over his own guffaws.

. . . five . . . four . . . three . . .

"Time-out!" yelled the quarterback, signaling a *T*.

On the sidelines, Ross was furious. "Have you all lost your minds? That was our last time-out!" He turned burning eyes on his hysterical running back. "Oh, that's *real* funny, Barry! What are you, a fifth grader?"

"But—but—," Elliot managed.

"I can be a funny guy too!" the coach bawled. "You want to hear my jokes? We lose on *Monday Night Football* with twenty million people watching! We miss the play-offs because of one game! We don't get a shot at the Superbowl! Am I hilarious, or what?"

It brought Elliot crashing back down to earth. "Sorry, Coach," he mumbled. "The guy's name . . ." There was no explaining it.

Ross slapped him on the shoulder. "Look, we've got

one last chance. Let's make it a good one."

There were two seconds remaining on the clock. Elliot got into his stance behind Scott Mitchell. *If we lose*, he thought miserably, *it'll be all my fault.* He gritted his teeth and forced the terrible notion from his head.

The tension was as dense as a black hole. *Monday Night Football*, do or die. For three fifth graders in Middletown, moments like this were the greatest thing in life. Elliot took that feeling and mixed it with the roar of the crowd to make the rocket fuel that would propel him one final yard.

"Hut!"

Cheering, screaming, shouting, grunting. Bodies smashed together. Elliot took the ball and launched himself at the goal line.

I can make it! I can see the end zone!

At the last second, a clean shirt stepped into the opening. O'Barfsky.

Wham! It was like running into a mountain. Elliot pushed hard, fighting with every last ounce of Barry Sanders's strength. But the angry lineman wouldn't budge.

Desperately, Elliot twisted away, leaping and dodging tacklers. He ran along the one yard line, trying to find a gap in the brick wall that was the Kansas City defense.

"... and the Chiefs are holding firm!" raved Al Michaels on *Monday Night Football*.

It's impossible! Elliot lamented. *I've lost the game for Detroit!*

And suddenly, he was looking right at it.

Daylight!

He stopped on a dime, spun around, and hurled himself up. With a cry of *"Lions!!"* he somersaulted in the air, avoiding a forest of grabbing arms.

Wump! He fell back to earth on the beautiful turf of the end zone.

The referee raised his hands. "Touchdown!"

The last thing Elliot saw was the huge form of the furious O'Barfsky, sailing through the air to land right on top of him.

In the Lighter TV room, Nick, Coleman, Hilary, and Barry Sanders leaped to their feet. *"Yes!!"* they cried in unison.

"Detroit wins!" bellowed Hilary.

"Detroit *ties*!" her brother shouted back. "But only after they kick the extra point!"

"Way to go, Sandy!" she screamed, throwing her arms out in celebration. Her left elbow conked Sanders right in the jaw, knocking him over. The all-pro running back went down like a sack of oats.

Bonk! His head smacked right into the secret weapon, wrapped up in Elliot's sleeping bag. Nick, Coleman, and Hilary were hugging each other. They never saw the tiny glowing football dancing over their companion.

"Get off me, you great big—" Elliot swallowed the rest of his sentence. O'Barfsky was gone; Arrowhead Stadium was gone. He was back with the Monday Night Football Club!

Coleman stared at him. "How can you lie down at a time like this? The Lions are going to tie it up!"

"But I've got to get back there!" cried Elliot. After leading Detroit to this amazing comeback, how could he miss out on overtime?

As he got to his feet, his arm got tangled in his bedroll. The sleeping bag lifted up, and the secret weapon fell out and hit the floor with a loud clunk. The tree trunk rolled over to the base of the TV and stopped. There it sat, broadcasting its carved message of love: H. L. & S. K.

"What the—," Hilary began.

"The secret weapon!" chorused Nick and Coleman.

Nick dove for it, but Hilary got there first. She picked it up and brandished it like a club.

"You," she told her brother, "are the lowest of the low. No, you're worse. You're the slimy slop the lowest of the low crawls around in. You and your Get-a-Life Club. You make me want to barf!"

Elliot snickered.

"Shut up!" And she stormed out of the TV room, tossing over her shoulder, "Go to sleep, doofus! You're supposed to be sick!"

"Way to go, Elliot," Nick accused. "All night we needed that stupid tree trunk. And you pick *now* to drop it at her feet."

"What was wrong with you?" put in Coleman. "When I asked for the secret weapon before, you looked at me like I was nuts."

"But, guys." Elliot defended himself. "It wasn't me."

"Then who was it?" snarled Nick. "The Easter Bunny?"

Elliot clutched at the scratchy material of the Eskimos jersey. "I was Barry Sanders! I've got to get back to the game for overtime!"

"You were *supposed* to be Barry Sanders," Coleman corrected. "But you wimped out."

"The shirt only works when you fall asleep," said Nick. "You were awake the whole time."

"But I *was* asleep," Elliot insisted. "While you guys

were doing homework! I was Barry Sanders! I gained a hundred and fifty yards in a thunderstorm! I scored two touchdowns! I laughed at the name O'Barfsky! Come on, would the real Barry Sanders do that? I'm the only one who cracks up at that kind of stuff! Quick—help me fall asleep again so I can get back to—"

He was interrupted by a cry from the TV.

"Bad snap!" exclaimed Al Michaels.

"What?!" The three boys wheeled to face the set. In the blowing wind and rain, the hiked ball flew right over the holder's head. Red jerseys swarmed the line of scrimmage. The Detroit kicker scrambled to pick up the ball, but was flattened by a stampede of Chiefs.

"The extra point is no good!" cried Al Michaels.

There would be no overtime. The Lions had lost a heartbreaker 20–19.

"No-o-o!!" howled Elliot.

Nick switched off the TV. "Too bad," he said, shaking his head. "They wasted one of Barry Sanders's best games ever."

"Too bad?!" repeated Elliot in disbelief. "I took hits that would have crushed a fifty-story building! I must have swallowed a half a gallon of mud! Every *inch* of that drive was won with blood and sweat and pain! It was the greatest thing I've ever been part of in my entire life! How could it all be for nothing?"

Nick crawled into his sleeping bag. "I know you're embarrassed about chickening out, Elliot. But you don't have to lie."

"If you can't trust the Monday Night Football Club, who *can* you trust?" added Coleman, turning out the light.

Oh, no! They didn't believe him! Having the game slip through his fingers was terrible enough. But to be snubbed by his two closest friends was the worst kind of agony. Elliot tossed and turned all night.

Too Cool, Out of Control, Awesome

Nick's bout with the chicken pox was over by Thanksgiving Day. So that morning, the Monday Night Football Club headed back to the school yard to try out the new and improved Pogo-Hat-Block Trampoline Punt Return.

They aced their trick play on the very first attempt. But Elliot didn't join in the high fives and postgame interviews. It still hurt that Nick and Coleman hadn't believed him about Monday night. He wasn't in a celebrating mood.

"Cheer up," Nick told him as they trudged through the fresh snow to the Rifkin house. "You can try it again next Monday. It's no big deal."

"I don't mind giving up my turn until you get it right," Coleman added soothingly.

"I *did* get it right," Elliot said stiffly.

As he ushered his friends inside, Elliot wondered if

this would be a sore point in the Monday Night Football Club from now on. He pictured the three of them at age eighty, watching *Monday Night Football* in the retirement community, still bickering over whether he had ever traded places with Barry Sanders way, way back in the twentieth century.

They poured themselves some juice, split the sports section into thirds, and sat down around the kitchen table with the newspaper.

Mrs. Rifkin appeared in the doorway. "Happy Thanksgiving, boys. Are you feeling better, Nick? Your skin has just about cleared up."

"I'm fine, thanks," Nick replied. "Nailed the Pogo-Hat-Block Trampoline Punt Return today."

"That's nice." Mrs. Rifkin tossed a letter onto the table in front of her son. "Elliot, this came for you yesterday. Who do you know in Missouri?"

"Nobody," said Elliot in confusion.

The packet was postmarked Kansas City. He waited until his mother had gone before tearing it open. A wide smile burst over his face like a brilliant sunrise. He had forgotten about this.

"What is it?" asked Coleman.

"Proof." Elliot pulled out a Polaroid photograph and placed it in front of his friends. It was the picture he had taken of himself in the locker room at halftime of *Monday Night Football*.

The snapshot showed a grinning Barry Sanders, holding up a hand-lettered sign: I AM ELLIOT RIFKIN!

Nick and Coleman stared in shock. They looked from the picture to Elliot and back to the picture again.

Nick was the first to break the silence. "Elliot, man, I am so sorry! I can't believe I doubted the word of a fellow Monday Night Club member."

"But you were wide awake," Coleman said hoarsely.

"That wasn't me," grinned Elliot. "It must have been Barry Sanders himself."

"He seemed so much like you," marveled Nick. "You know, kind of quiet—"

"You'd be quiet, too," Elliot pointed out, "if you were a famous football star, and *poof*, you ended up in the body of an eleven-year-old, watching yourself on TV. You'd be pretty freaked out."

Nick snapped his fingers. "That explains why you went so nuts over the missed extra point. It was your game! Sorry the Lions lost."

Elliot shook his head. "I was upset at first. But then I thought, losing is part of football too. I mean, every single NFL game has ninety fantastic athletes. Half of them always go home disappointed. The important thing is to be out there playing the greatest game in the world with the best in the business! I wouldn't swap last Monday for a million blowout wins!"

All at once, Coleman turned pale. "I was *mean* to Barry Sanders when he was you! I kept bugging him to fall asleep."

Nick chuckled. "Don't worry about Barry Sanders. He's got his old self back, and he's ready to roll through defenses and break records, same as always."

"Don't count on it," said Elliot. He pointed to a small article at the bottom of the sports section. The headline read SANDERS TO MISS ANNUAL THANKSGIVING GAME DUE TO CHICKEN POX.

"Chicken pox?" mused Nick. "How could he get chicken pox?"

"From *you*," Coleman explained. "Right? He was with you for all of *Monday Night Football*."

"It was okay for Coleman and me to be there because we've already had chicken pox," Elliot added. "But I guess Barry Sanders never had it—until now."

"Aw, man, this stinks!" moaned Nick. "I'm the biggest football fan on earth, and what do I do? I give a child-hood disease to one of the best players in history! How could it be worse?"

"Listen to this." Elliot began to read from the paper:

"Sanders is confident that he can put the time off to good use. He hopes to develop a new play for the Lions' offense. "'I got the idea last Monday night,' he told reporters. "I call it the 'Heavy Artillery Sweep.'"

"Heavy Artillery?" repeated Nick in dismay. "That's my stupid sister! She gave him that play during Monday Night Football Club!"

"It's not fair," Coleman complained. "We watch every game, every drive, every *snap*, and *Hilary* gets to design a play for the Detroit Lions!"

Nick threw up his arms. "Who knew that was Barry Sanders and not Elliot? I mean, how can you tell? I wish we could have seen the switch happen."

Elliot looked thoughtful. "Maybe you can."

"Are you nuts?" snapped Coleman. "It was three days ago."

"I just remembered." Elliot sat forward in excitement. "When I tried out the shirt last weekend, I videotaped myself!" He leaped up and ran for the stairs.

Nick and Coleman were hot on his heels.

The cassette, marked LETA '97, was still in Mr. Rifkin's camera. Elliot popped it into the VCR in his parents' bedroom and hit Play. He fast-forwarded past his great-aunt's lipstick-bomb kisses, and cousin Leonard's antics with his whoopie cushions.

"Right there!" cried Nick.

Elliot slowed the tape to normal speed. There he was, suffering the itchiness of the Eskimos jersey, with Leonard's joy buzzer taped to his chest.

The Monday Night Football Club watched in fascination as Elliot grew drowsy. His eyelids drooped, and his head began to roll backward.

"Hey," Coleman observed. "You look really goofy when you fall asleep."

"Shhh!" hissed Elliot. "Pay attention."

"Wait a minute," said Nick. "What's that?"

The three stared in amazement as the tiny glowing football appeared above Elliot's face. It began to move slowly.

"Is it a firefly?" asked Coleman.

Elliot hit Pause. The members of the Monday Night Football Club crawled up to the TV screen where the light was frozen an inch from the tip of Elliot's nose.

"A football!" they all shouted at the same time.

"But why does it bounce around like that?" wondered Nick.

Elliot hit Rewind. "I've got it!" he cried. "Watch what the light does when I play it fast-forward."

He hit Cue. The glowing football raced through its dance, leaving streaks of light that mapped out its path over the sleeping Elliot.

"Twenty!" chorused the Monday Night Club.

"Barry Sanders's number!" Nick exclaimed. "I get it. The football spells out the number of the player you're switching with!"

"Amazing!" marveled Coleman.

"It's way better than amazing," breathed Elliot. "It's too cool, out of control, awesome! It's—it's *magic!*"

"I thought you didn't believe in magic," Coleman pointed out.

"You said everything has a logical explanation."

Elliot backed up the tape. "The explanation is there *is* no explanation."

"That's not very scientific," put in Nick.

"Sure it is," argued Elliot. "I set out to prove that there's no such thing as magic, and I ended up proving I was wrong." He shut off the TV. "Now you guys better get out of here. I have to write my fantasy story before Mrs. Montrose flunks me."

"What's it going to be about?" asked Nick.

"What else?" grinned Elliot. "Some lucky guy who turns into his favorite football player. It's the *ultimate* fantasy!"

Monday Night Football Club Story of the Incredible Barry Sanders

Few running backs in NFL history have been as successful or as elusive as Detroit's Barry Sanders. In 1997, his ninth season, he could become the league's second all-time rusher with more than 12,000 yards. Since coming from Oklahoma State as the 1988 Heisman Trophy winner, the three-time NFL rushing champion has been consistently excellent.

In 1996, he became the first player to rush for at least 1,000 yards in eight consecutive seasons. While the numbers tell part of the story, what makes Sanders so great are his moves and his speed. Few other players can make tacklers miss like Sanders does. And even fewer can catch him in a downfield footrace.

Barry Sanders grew up in Wichita, Kansas, where he not only was a football star but also played basketball, even though at five feet nine inches, he was short for that game. At Oklahoma State, he set a school record with fifty-six touchdowns. In 1988, after leading the nation in rushing with an NCAA-record 2,628 yards, he won the Heisman Trophy as college football's best player. The Lions chose Sanders with the third pick of the 1989 NFL draft. He was a superstar from the first time he stepped onto an NFL field. He was the rookie of the year in 1989 and went to the first of his eight Pro Bowls.

As a rookie, he was just ten yards short of winning the NFL

rushing title. In 1990, he became the rushing champion, gaining 1,304 yards. In 1991, he led the league in touchdowns with seventeen and helped the Lions reach the NFC Championship Game. Barry had his greatest NFL season in 1994, gaining an NFL-best 1,883 yards, the fourth-highest total ever. In 1996, Barry was the NFL rushing champion for the third time with 1,553 yards. He gained 175 yards in the final game of the season to earn the title. He also became the first player to rush for more than 1,500 yards for three consecutive seasons.

Off the field, Barry helps the Special Olympics. He also enjoys spending time with his son, Barry Jr., age three.

BARRY'S BEST

Eight Pro Bowls / 1989 NFL rookie of the year / 1991 NFL/AP NFC player of the year / 1990, 1994, 1996 NFL rushing champion / 1994 AP offensive player of the year.

SANDERS BY THE NUMBERS

	Att.	Ydg.	TDs	Rec.	Ydg.	TDs
1996	307	1,553	11	24	147	0
Career	2,384	11,725	84	281	2,309	7

The United Negro College Fund

A United Negro College Fund education can be the most important thing in a life.

Unfortunately, not all young people have the same chances to go to college. The United Negro College Fund (UNCF) helps young people make their dream of a college degree come true. I'm proud to be one of fifty NFL players who have entered the UNCF Golden Circle. We all recognize that being a star in the classroom is more important than being a star on the field.

Through UNCF, we are able to help young African-Americans from all over the nation attend college. UNCF also assists historically black colleges by providing scholarships for deserving students. UNCF has been doing this important work since 1944. I'm very happy that I can be a small part of its success. You can, too, either by donating to the UNCF or by applying for a scholarship when you reach college age.

For more information, please write to United Negro College Fund, 8260 Willow Oak Corp. Dr., Fairfax, VA 22031. Tell them Barry Sanders sent you!

NFL/MONDAY NIGHT FOOTBALL CLUB FANTASY SWEEPSTAKES OFFICIAL RULES

NO PURCHASE NECESSARY

1. HOW TO ENTER: Handprint full name and address (city, state or province and zip or mail code), daytime phone number with area code and birthdate on a 3" x 5" card; on a separate sheet of paper write an original story about a football fantasy no longer than 200 words; staple the card to the upper right corner of the first page of the story and mail it, postage prepaid, to NFL/Monday Night Football Club Fantasy Sweepstakes, 114 Fifth Avenue, New York, NY 10011, postmarked by February 2, and received by February 6, 1998.

2. ENTRY LIMITATIONS: Limit one entry per person. Story must be an original work and hand printed or typed. Entries which meet all the requirements will be eligible for the sweepstakes drawing. Open only to children between 7 and 14 upon entering who are legal residents of the U.S.A. (excluding its territories, possessions, overseas military installations and commonwealths) or Canada (excluding Quebec) and not employees of Disney Publishing, (the "Sponsor"), The National Football League, their parent, subsidiary or affiliated companies, the advertising, promotional or fulfillment agencies of any of them, nor members of their immediate families. Sponsor is not responsible for printing errors or inaccurate, incomplete, stolen, lost, illegible, mutilated, postage-due, misdirected, delayed or late entries or mail, or equipment or telephone malfunction.

3. RESERVATIONS: Void where prohibited or restricted by law and subject to all federal, state, provincial and local laws and regulations. All entries become the Sponsor's property and will not be returned. By entering this sweepstakes, each entrant agrees to be bound by these rules and the decisions of the judges. Acceptance of prize constitutes the grant of an unconditional right to use winner's name, picture, voice and/or likeness for any and all publicity, advertising and promotional purposes without additional compensation, except where prohibited by law. Sponsor is not responsible for claims, injuries, losses or damages of any kind resulting from the acceptance, use, misuse, possession, loss or misdirection of the prize.

4.WINNER: Will be notified by mail after February 14, 1997. Prize will be awarded in the name of the parent/legal guardian of the winner. Winner is required to prove eligibility. The failure of a potential winner's parent/legal guardian to verify address and execute and return an Affidavit of Eligibility/Release within ten (10) days from the date of notification, or the return of a notification as undeliverable, will result in disqualification and the selection of an alternate winner. All travelers will be required to execute a Release of Liability prior to ticketing. A Canadian resident who is a winner will be required to correctly answer a mathematical skills test to be eligible to collect the prize. For the name of winner (after February 14, 1998) and/or sweepstakes rules, send a self-addressed, stamped envelope to NFL/Monday Night Football Club Fantasy Sweepstakes, 114 Fifth Avenue, New York, NY 10011. WA and VT residents may omit the return postage.

5.PROCEDURES: Sweepstakes begins on September 15, 1997, and ends on February 2, 1998. Winner will be selected from all eligible entries received in a random drawing on or about February 14, 1998, under the supervision of the Marketing Division of Hyperion Books for Children as judges. Odds of winning depend on the number of eligible entries received.

6.PRIZE: One (1) GRAND PRIZE: A four (4) days/three(3) nights trip for four (4) to the 1998 NFL Quarterback Challenge (the "Event"). The date and location of the Event is yet to be determined by The National Football League. The trip includes VIP seating in players' hospitality area for one (1) day at the Event, coach air transportation to/from the major metropolitan airport nearest to winner's home and the major airport nearest the Event, airport transfers and hotel accommodations (one room) for three (3) nights in the city of the Event. All taxes and expenses not mentioned herein are not included and are the responsibility of the winner. Winner must be willing to make the trip during the Event, or an alternate winner will be selected. (Approximate retail value of trip: $2,000.) Prize is not redeemable for cash or transferable and no substitution allowed except at the sole discretion of the Sponsor, who may substitute a prize of equal or greater value if the Event is cancelled for any reason. The prize will be awarded.

NFL Films, Inc., NFL Properties, Inc., NFL Enterprises, L.P., the NFL, its member professional football teams ("Member Clubs") and each of their respective affiliates, officers, directors, agents, and employees (collectively, "the NFL") will have no liability or responsibility for any claim arising in connection with participation in this sweepstakes or offer or any prize awarded. The NFL has not offered or sponsored this sweepstakes in any way.

Enter the NFL/Monday Night Football Club Fantasy Sweepstakes

What's your football fantasy?

Tell us your story and turn fantasy into reality.

- Being the receiver to John Elway's quarterback?
- Passing to Barry Sanders AND escaping the sack?
- Calling the plays in a Super Bowl huddle?
- Getting drafted by your favorite pro NFL team?

Grand Prize:

An all-expense-paid trip to the Footaction NFL Quarterback Challenge for a chance to see your favorite NFL football players in action!

Here's the Game Plan:

Tell us your football fantasy in 200 words or less (printed or typed).

Attach a 3x5 card with your name, address, city, state, zip code, and birthdate to the upper right corner of the first page of your story.

Mail to NFL/Monday Night Football Club Fantasy Sweepstakes, 114 Fifth Avenue, New York, NY 10011.

Make sure your entry is postmarked no later that February 2, 1998.

You must be at least 7 years old but not older than 14 by February 2, 1998 to enter.

Hot Hint On How To Score: Give your fantasy a reality check—incorporate real players and places into your story!

NFL YOUTH PROGRAMS

NFL Flag presented by Nike

Get into flag football competition with the NFL Flag program.
Competitive leagues and instruction are divided into appropriate age
groups for boys and girls age 6–14.
Leagues take place in the fall and spring in Arizona, Carolina,
Chicago, Cincinnati, Cleveland, Dallas, Denver, Jacksonville, Kansas City,
Miami, New England, Philadelphia, and San Diego.

For information how to get involved, Call 1-800-NFL-SNAP

Gatorade NFL Punt, Pass & Kick
September 1997

How far can you throw a football? Can you connect with your receiver?
How far can you kick it? Can you send it sailing through the
middle of the goal post? Show off your football talents at the country's
largest skills competition for boys and girls ages 8–15.

For more information on the competition nearest you, call 1-800-NFL-SNAP

Scholastic NFL Flag presented by Nike and
NFL Gatorade Punt, Pass & Kick
September and October 1997

So, you want to play football during P. E. classes?
You can, as you learn the skills needed to play the game and win.
Ask your physical education teachers to get involved—it's fun and it's free!
The NFL Flag takes place in Arizona, Carolina, Chicago, Cinncinnati,
Cleveland, Dallas, Denver, Jacksonville, Kansas City, Miami,
New England, Philadelphia, and San Diego.
The NFL Gatorade Punt, Pass & Kick takes place in Atlanta, Minnesota,
New Orleans, San Diego, San Francisco, and Tampa Bay.

Kmart NFL Family Days

Boys and Girls ages 8–15, listen up and win! Three hundred lucky families
of four in each of the cities below will have the chance to get on the field
and go behind the scenes with Kmart NFL Family Days. Go right into
your local stadium for a day of interactive clinics, coaches chats, insider
tours and more. Camps take place in Carolina, Dallas, Detroit,
Jacksonville, New York (Jets), Oakland, and Washington
during weeks 3–10 of the NFL season.

For registration information, contact your local Kmart.

Suit up for the big game in official NFL gear

When Elliot switches places with Barry Sanders during Monday Night Football, he's got to have his head in the game. Now you can get your head in the game too with this exclusive offer for an official NFL Player Name Cap.

Player Number

Adjustable

Direct Embroidered Player Name

ficial Team Colors

Join the hottest teams around!

Score an NFL Fan Packet today!

Get the scoop on all your favorite players with your own NFL Fan Packet! Filled with the hot inside info you can't get anywhere else, this exclusive packet includes the NFL's Play Football Calendar, plus lots of great extras.

For your free NFL Fan Packet, send your name and address and favorite team name to the following address:

NFL Fan Packet
Starline Sports Marketing
1480 Terrell Rd., Marietta, GA 3006

Get off the sidelines and onto the field with NFL.COM

NFL.COM is the official website of the National Football league and the ultimate on-line destination for football fans. From late-breaking news to comprehensive team profiles to live scores and play-by-play every Game Day, NFL.COM covers it all. Fans can interact with their favorite players, sound off in polls and chat about the "big game." And beginning with the 1997 season, a brand new section devoted to kids—Play Football!—will make its debut. Filled with fun games, stats, and trivia, the Play Football! area will be hot! Check it out.

Check out NFL.COM for links to the Monday Night Football Club to find out which football star the guys will switch with next!

Join the hottest team around!

The Monday Night Football Club 1997-1998 Schedule

Available Now
Monday Night Football Club #1
The Quarterback Exchange:
I Was John Elway
ISBN 0-7868-1236-2

Monday Night Football Club #2
The Running Back Conversion:
I Was Barry Sanders
ISBN 0-7868-1237-0

November 1997
Monday Night Football Club #3
The Super Bowl Switch:
I Was Dan Marino
ISBN 0-7868-1238-9

January 1998
Monday Night Football Club #4
Heavy Artillery:
I Was Junior Seau
ISBN 0-7868-1259-1

Look for new books coming down the field every other month!

Watch this!

Every book comes packed with coupons and 800-numbers for exclusive NFL offers on official football jerseys, hats, shirts, shorts and other gear plus free stuff from the league and lots of inside stuff you can't get anywhere else.

Available at your local bookstore

$4.95 each